AF584305

Published by Scholastic Australia in 2022.

Scholastic Australia Pty Limited
PO Box 579 Gosford NSW 2250
ABN 11 000 614 577
www.scholastic.com.au

Part of the Scholastic Group
Sydney • Auckland • New York • Toronto • London • Mexico City • New Delhi
Hong Kong • Buenos Aires • Puerto Rico

ISBN 978-1-76120-556-9

Printed in China by RR Donnelley.

Scholastic Australia's policy, in association with RR Donnelley, is to use papers that are renewable and made efficiently from wood grown in responsibly managed forests, so as to minimise its environmental footprint.

10 9 8 7 6 5 4 3 2 1 22 23 24 25 26 / 2

MARVEL

AVENGERS MECH STRIKE

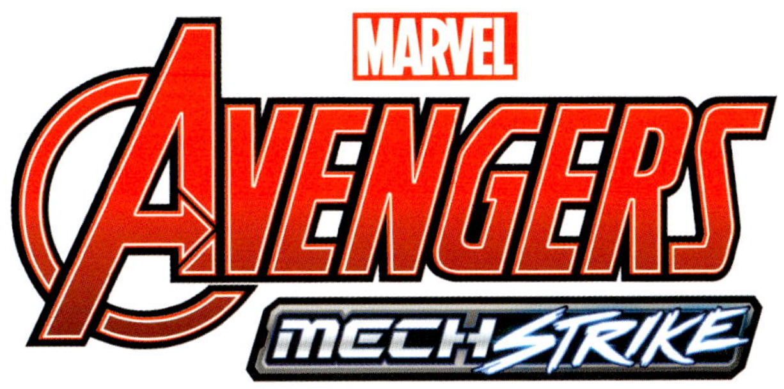

HEROES TO THE CORE

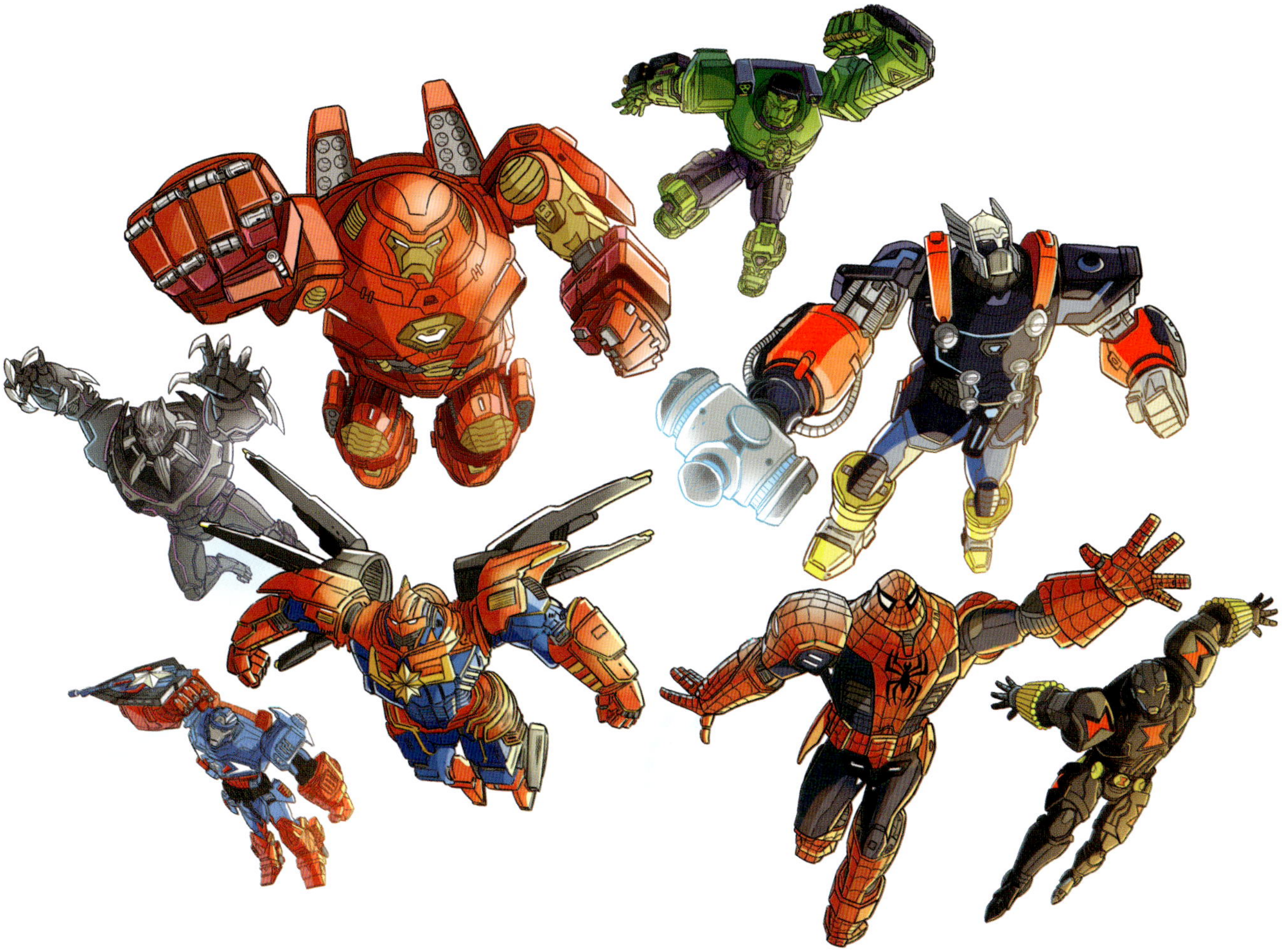

Written by **JEREMY WHITLEY**

Illustrated by **STEVE KURTH, ANDREA GREPPI AND MARIA CLAUDIA DIGENOVA**

SCHOLASTIC

SYDNEY AUCKLAND NEW YORK TORONTO LONDON MEXICO CITY
NEW DELHI HONG KONG BUENOS AIRES PUERTO RICO

In the streets of New York City, a strange creature rampaged.

It chased civilians. It ate cars and buildings. It was called the **BIOMECHANOID.**

The city needed help. The city needed heroes. The city needed . . .

. . . THE AVENGERS.

Iron Man, Thor and Captain Marvel fly to the rescue. Black Panther and Black Widow take to the rooftops. Captain America and Spider-Man fly aboard the Quinjet.

Aboard the **QUINJET,** Captain America called out orders. 'Thor and Captain Marvel are the heavy hitters; they'll take the lead on the attack. Everyone else, our first priority is to clear out those civilians.'

Thor held his hammer, **MJOLNIR,** out towards the Biomechanoid and shouted, 'Creature, you face the son of Odin! You shall yield.'

Captain Marvel joined in, blasting glowing plasma from her hands, but the creature just grew larger. 'He doesn't seem to be yielding. Cap, I think it's time to call in the big guy.'

'That's a go for Hulk, Doctor Banner,' Captain America called.

On a rooftop overlooking the fight, an average-looking man in a coat sighed. 'He says that like it's easy.'

Seconds later, bulging green muscles ripped his clothing to shreds from the inside as the man transformed from Doctor Bruce Banner into the Incredible Hulk.

'HULK SMASH!' Hulk screamed as he leapt from the building onto the Biomechanoid. Hulk hit the creature with all of his might.

But something strange happened. The Biomechanoid didn't get smashed. It grabbed Hulk.

'Cap, I don't like the readings I'm getting off of this thing,' said Iron Man. 'Not only did he absorb Captain Marvel's energy, now he's pulling the gamma radiation right out of Hulk.'

'If it feeds off of energy, I think I have a plan,' Black Panther called from the nearby rooftop. 'Spider-Man and Black Widow, get Banner. I will handle the creature.'

Spider-Man swung Doctor Banner away with his webbing while Black Widow used her stinger to cover them.

'We've got him, Black Panther,' Black Widow reported.

'He's smaller, but he still smells green and sweaty,' Spider-Man added.

Black Panther took a running leap and jumped straight at the creature's giant jaws. The Biomechanoid saw him coming and opened wide.

The massive jaws snapped shut and Black Panther was gone! The Avengers gaped on in shock.

'Everybody stay clear of that thing,' Captain America ordered. 'It just ate Black Panther whole.'

The Biomechanoid began twitching and twisting. **'KEEP BACK!'** Captain America shouted, 'We don't know what it's doing.'

The Biomechanoid EXPLODED!
Pieces of the creature flew everywhere.
All that was left once the smoke cleared was Black Panther, standing where the Biomechanoid had been, the creature's core in his hand. 'The creature couldn't stomach the taste of Vibranium,' Black Panther said.

For days, Tony Stark and T'Challa examined the core at Avengers Mountain. Finally, they called a meeting of the Avengers to tell them what they had found.

‘Each of you will be equipped with one of these wristbands, each with its own laser,’ T’Challa began.

‘Ummm . . .’ Spider-Man interrupted, ‘Black Widow and I already have fancy wrist jewellery and, also, how are tiny bracelet lasers going to stop those things?’

Iron Man smiled. **‘LET US SHOW YOU.’**

Iron Man and Black Panther led the Avengers into a large hangar bay where a surprise awaited.

'These are your **MECH STRIKE** exoskeletons, designed to work with your strengths and powers,' Iron Man explained. 'Your wristbands connect you to your exoskeleton.'

Spider-Man stuck out his hand eagerly. 'Okay, I can wear two bracelets if it means I get a mech.'

Just then, **ALARMS SOUNDED.**

'It appears we have an opportunity for a test run,' Black Panther declared. 'New Biomechanoids have attacked.'

'You heard the man,' Captain America said. 'Get your wrist units and mech up. We've got a world to save.'

AVENGERS ASSEMBLE!

Captain America and Spider-Man found a Biomechanoid in a junkyard in Tallahassee, Florida.

'Aww man, why do I always get fights in junkyards and sewers?' Spider-Man groaned, using the super strong cables from his suit to web the creature up.

'CONCENTRATE, Spider-Man,' Cap commanded, hitting the creature with his mech's giant shield. 'This thing's been eating all sorts of scraps. We can't let him get loose.'

Thor and Black Widow found a Biomechanoid on the rooftops of Kiev, Ukraine.

'Halt, villain!' Thor shouted, attacking. The creature caught Thor's mech. The mech swung its hammer with all of its might, but Thor couldn't get loose.

The Biomechanoid didn't see Black Widow's mech sneak up behind it and scan it. 'I've got a lock on the core,' Black Widow said, 'I'm bringing this thing down.' She fired the rockets from her mech's wrist.

Captain Marvel and Doctor Banner found the third new Biomechanoid in Montreal, Canada. With its first swipe, the Biomechanoid nearly destroyed Doctor Banner's mech, but Captain Marvel swooped in to save him.

'Banner,' Captain Marvel called. 'The mechs work with our powers. You need to **HULK OUT!'** Turning into Hulk made the mech double in size, too strong for any Biomechanoid to face.

'QUICK!' Iron Man yelled, 'take its memory core while I've got it pinned.'

In Tianjin, China, Black Panther dug the claws of his mech deep into the Biomechanoid and pulled out the memory core.

'We have to get back,' T'Challa said with concern, looking at the memory core in his hands. 'There will be more, and we must be sure that the others have been victorious as well.'

When Iron Man and Black Panther returned to Avengers Mountain, they were happy to find everyone else there too, celebrating their victory.

But Tony and T'Challa knew Biomechanoids would attack again. It was time to plan their next battle!